Animal Sensors

Greg Pyers

CONTENTS

Rigby

What's Happening?

We all have **sensors** that tell us what is happening around us. We can smell, feel, taste, see, and hear.

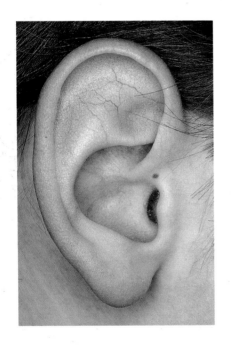

How do animals know what is happening around them?

They have sensors like our eyes, ears, and noses, but many animals have other sensors, such as **antennae** and whiskers.

whiskers

antenna

beak

bill

Big Ears

Some bats hunt for insects at night.

How do bats find their food?

In the dark, bats use their ears more than their eyes to find food.

When a bat flies, it makes sounds that are like very high squeals. These sounds bounce back from flying insects. The bat's large ears hear the **echo**. The bat then flies toward the echo to catch its meal.

Night Eyes

Cats are excellent nighttime hunters. Even in the dark, a cat is able to see its **prey**.

How does a cat see so well at night?

Look at a cat's eyes. The black slits in the center of the eyes are called the **pupils**. The pupils let light into the eyes. At night, when there is little light, the pupils open very wide. So even though it is dark, enough light enters the cat's eyes to see tiny animals like mice.

Super Nose

A salmon returns from the ocean to the stream where it was born to lay its eggs.

How does a salmon find its way back to the stream where it was born?

The salmon uses its nose to smell the water of its own stream.

Just think—thousands of streams pour into the ocean, yet each salmon can find just the right stream. What a nose!

Swiveling Eyes

A chameleon hunts for insects. It can see above or below and behind or ahead at the same time.

How can a chameleon see all around?

A chameleon has eyes that swivel. While one eye can look for insects above or behind, the other can look ahead or below. When one eye spots an insect, the other eye turns to see the insect, too. The lizard can then judge the distance for its sticky tongue to strike.

Picking Up Signals

To mate, a male moth must find a female moth. A female moth is small, and may be miles away.

A moth can't hear or see very far, so how does a male moth find a female moth?

The female moth sprays a chemical **signal** into the air. When even just a few drops of the chemical are caught by the male moth's large, feathery antennae, he can follow the scent and find her.

Fish with Feeling

A fish can sense water movement. In this way, it knows best where to swim.

How does a fish do this?

Along each side of a fish's body is a line of touch sensors. These are called the **lateral lines**. With its lateral lines, the fish feels water movements made by other fish swimming.

lateral line

If a shark is near, a fish's lateral lines will **detect** lots of water movement. The fish then knows it has to hurry away.

Sensitive Beak

The ibis feeds on worms and insects that live hidden underground.

How does an ibis find this food when it cannot see, smell, or hear it?

The ibis has a long, **sensitive** beak. To find its food, the ibis pokes its beak deep into soft soil and mud. When its sensitive beak touches a frog, a worm, or an insect burrowing underground, the ibis snaps it up.

Feeling the Heat

Rattlesnakes often hunt prey, such as mice, on dark nights. A rattlesnake has no ears and very poor eyesight.

heat-sensing pit

So *how does a rattlesnake know where its prey is?*

People can feel the warmth of a heater on their skin. A rattlesnake can feel the heat from a mouse using the two pits on the front of its head. In the dark, a rattlesnake can't hear or see a mouse, but the pits tell it exactly where the mouse is.

Electric Sense

The platypus hunts on creek bottoms for shrimps, worms, and insects. When it hunts, the platypus closes its eyes and ears.

How does a platypus find food?

When a shrimp or other creature moves, its muscles send off **electricity**. The bill of the platypus is an electrical sensor. The platypus sweeps its rubbery bill from side to side to detect the shrimp's electricity. In this way, the platypus is guided to its food.

Conclusion

Our sensors tell us what is going on around us. But do they detect everything? What if we had extra sensors, like those of the animals in this book?

Imagine being able to detect electricity, like a platypus can with its bill, or to detect body heat, like a rattlesnake can with its pits. Imagine how the world would seem to us then.

Glossary

antennae sensors that are found on the heads of insects and other small animals

detect to discover

echo a sound that bounces back to your ears

electricity a type of energy

lateral lines a line of sensors on each side of a fish

prey an animal that is eaten by another animal

pupil the black part in the center of an eye

sensitive having the power to detect movement or change

sensor part of an animal that detects things; for example, ears are sensors that detect sounds

signal a sign that is sent as a message to another living thing

Index